HUNT FOR NAGAMANI

DR. VIKAS SIVADASAN

Dedicated to my beloved parents

Contents

About the Author

Dr. Vikas Sivadasan, a Keralite, spent his childhood in Pilani, Rajasthan, and Jabalpur, Madhya Pradesh, India.

He did his schooling abroad, in Addis Ababa. After completing 12th Grade, he joined for commercial pilot training. He did Aircraft Maintenance Engineering, BAMS (Bachelor of Ayurveda Medicine and Surgery) and Diploma in Clinical Siddha Practices.

Currently he is practicing as a Medical Doctor (Ayurveda).

Also the same author has:

Alien in the Backyard

Ethiopian Opal

Acknowledgements

- Mum - Thank you for your invaluable help and suggestions.
- Dad - Thank you for your wonderful feedback.
- Notion press – Thank you for providing all the assistance and publishing this book.
- The entire marketing, sales and production teams - Thank you for all your help.

I

Dr. Binoy at work

Dr. Binoy Nambiar was rushing to the university as his car had broken down half way to the university. He got into a local bus. Normal times he would have hated to get into a local bus as it's always tightly packed and one can hardly breathe. But he had no other option as he was already half an hour late for his lecture. As soon as he got down the bus, he rushed to the class room, sweating.

By seeing the Professor, all students stood up and wished him, "Good morning Professor", in chorus. He asked them to sit down.

He delivered his lecture on excavation using a chalk piece and black board and a few research papers. He was quite old-fashioned and didn't believe in teaching with OHP slides, projectors and laptops. Moreover, recent studies had proven that teaching with OHP and laptops resulted in students grasping very little, compared to the old fashioned way of lecturing with chalk on black board. He wrapped up his lecture in 2 hours, gave assignment to the students and cautioned them to complete it by next week, as the marks would be added to the mid -term exam marks.

Dr. Binoy went to his cabin in the office, sipped his usual cup of tea and had a tablet for his blood pressure. All the office work was taking a toll on him which sky-rocketed his blood pressure every now and then. As he got to work, he received a call from his wife reminding him to have his blood pressure pills on time. He told her not to worry as he already had the pills and feeling much better. Dr. Binoy got down to preparing MCQ (Multiple Choice Questions) exam papers for his students for the upcoming mid-term test, next week. Dr. Binoy was also head of the department of Archeology, so he has to supervise other lecturers' work too. He told them to be ready with handouts for their respective subjects which they were supposed to lecture on, before the starting of next semester. Dr. Binoy was very strict and maintained proper decorum both in the office and the classroom. At 5 PM when the lecture got over, he packed his bag and called a cab back to his home. As soon as he reached home, he was welcomed by his wife. He planted a kiss on her cheek and greeted her. He went to his room, had a bath and sat down to do his evening prayers. It was 7 PM when he finished his prayers. The doorbell rang. A few students were waiting in line in front of the door.

He told them, "Come in and take your seat."

He told his wife, "Make some tea, honey."

Dr. Binoy used to take free classes for the talented students coming from poor families. He also had many students doing Ph.D under him. He didn't mind teasing them a little and made them do his household work for free, like buying vegetables from the market, servicing his car, pushing the car from behind when it showed delay in starting, refueling his car once in a while, driving him to college every now and then. If they don't do his house hold work, he never accepted their thesis and made them keep resubmitting their thesis. Students doing Ph.D under Dr. Binoy could finish their Ph.D within a span of minimum 10-15 years.

Next day morning, Dr. Binoy called up one of his PhD students to ride him in his car to the university, as usual. The Ph.D student came on time and drove the professor to the university and reached on time as he was scared that any delay in reaching the university would further delay the completion of his Ph.D.

Dr. Binoy got to the principal's office, opened the MCQ booklets and brought it to the classroom.

Students wished the professor, "Good morning", in chorus but were very nervous about the test as Dr. Binoy was known to prepare tough question papers which only he could ace.

Dr. Binoy said, "You have only one hour to solve the MCQs. Any foul play will result in barring you for a year; moreover a heavy fine will also be imposed."

Students attended their examination in pin drop silence. Clearing Dr. Binoy's paper was like attaining 'moksha' (salvation) for the students. Dr. Binoy collected the MCQ booklets along with the assignments he had given them last week.

Dr. Binoy told, "I expect good results."

He added, "I am also looking forward to flunk those who didn't submit their assignments."

He got home in the evening from work, greeted his wife by kissing her, as usual, and started his remaining routine work of the day. To this, his wife became very angry.

She almost yelled, "Do you remember today's importance? Today is our marriage anniversary."

He cancelled his free classes that night and told the students to come back the next day as he is busy with some office work.

He said, "Sorry darling."

She whispered, "What a workaholic I got married to!"

Soon after they left, he took his wife for outing. He drove her to the nearest shopping mall and brought her a saree of designer wear. Then he took her for a candle light dinner in a fancy hotel. Finally his wife forgave him and enjoyed the dinner together and went home happily with the Professor.

II

Dr. Binoy finds Nagarjun

Next day morning, Professor received a call from the US, from the Dean of College of Business Administration. It was about his son Vijay. The Dean complained about his son's irregularity in college and that he had been flunking his exams as well. Dr. Binoy humbly requested the Dean to bear with his son as it is probably homesickness and his son is finding it difficult to adjust with the American culture there. Little did he know that Vijay was flunking exams and being irregular only to make money by winning illegal races in the US, which, by the way, he is quite good at.

After talking to the Dean, Dr. Binoy called up Vijay in the US and fired him thoroughly on phone.

He shouted, "Clear the exam or never think of coming back home."

On the other hand, the principal of the university called Dr. Binoy to his office.

He said, "Professor, I think you are overloaded. Why can't you appoint an assistant?"

"You are right sir. Too much work load." Dr. Binoy agreed.

"Inform the administration to advertise the post of an assistant for you, Professor." Principal said.

"Sure sir. So nice of you." Dr. Binoy expressed his gratitude.

Soon an interview for the post of assistant was conducted.

Participants who came for the interview were really dumb or were not at all suitable for the post. Finally, he met a candidate named Pooja suitable for the post. Her CV was top notch. She had graduated with distinction. She has good communication skills and had a vibrant personality.

He selected her for the post, congratulated her, "Congrats! Pooja, can you join tomorrow itself?"

She nodded in the affirmative.

He further said, "I was looking forward to work with someone of your talent and caliber."

On Pooja's day of joining, Dr. Binoy provided her with a personal table and chair to work. He handed over her some computer typing work as she had good computer skills mentioned in her CV. She was happy to work on computer as typing was a piece of cake for her. Her typing speed was 85 words/ minute.

Ever since Dr. Binoy appointed a lady assistant, his wife was quite suspicious of him and kept on calling him in between to keep a check on him, even when Dr. Binoy told her that Pooja is just his colleague and nothing beyond that.

Dr Binoy was soon assigned work on an excavation site at Bhedaghat, in Jabalpur. He went with Pooja right away to the excavation site. He found Jabalpur a very busy city with lot of pollution. But Bhedaghat was a peaceful place with a lot of greenery around. Nearby flows the Narmada

River which was considered pious in the Hindu mythology. People believed that dipping in the Narmada River is auspicious. Visitors from far off used to book tourist buses in advance to come there. People believed it auspicious to flow the ashes of their beloved departed souls in the Narmada River.

Bhedaghat was filled with precious marble rocks. Tourists also could pick up a few marble stones to carry as a souvenir on their returning home. Localites were busy selling various statues carved out beautifully of marble on stalls on the side ways. It was truly a form of art wherever one glanced.

A bit far was Dhuandhar falls. Unlike normal water falls, this water fall appeared a lot smoky and misty as the water fall was flowing from a great height of 30 meters. This resulted in creating a misty water fall there. It was also a tourist site. The marble rocks appeared silvery under the moon light. The valley of white marble appeared yellow during sunsets. Tourists also enjoyed boat rides in the Narmada River.

Professor's excavation site was nearby. Professor got his men to dig as quickly as they could. He verified with Pooja the location of the excavation site and told her to note any findings they may come across. He also told her to take pictures of the site and make a soft copy of it.

Weeks passed since the professor's men kept digging at the site. Suddenly, they came across an underground tunnel. Professor told that no one should enter the tunnel without his permission. He told Pooja to inform their headquarters about the tunnel they had found. He decided to go by himself and inspect the underground tunnel. He went with a torch and archeological equipment in his backpack inside the tunnel. The tunnel was quite deep and went in a zig zag direction underground. He could notice some markings on the tunnel walls. He came near and took a close look in the torch light. To his surprise, the marking showed a map to the hidden Naga village of which he had heard only rumors. The Professor immediately noted down every minute detail of the map and wiped off the markings on the tunnel so that the map remained a secret from the outside world. Next day, the professor allowed Pooja and other archeologists to enter the tunnel to take samples and photos.

He instructed Pooja, "Make a soft copy of the findings. I have to leave the site as some urgent matter had come up."

Dr. Binoy decided to find the Naga village on his own based on the map he had found in the tunnel underground.

After a week, Dr. Binoy embarked on a journey in the dense jungle of the Kanha forest and followed the route map closely. His land cruiser was bullet proof and had all the latest technologies and equipments required for such an expedition through the forest. Dr. Binoy stopped his car near a hill. He started climbing the hill with his trekking equipment, reached up the hill. He found a temple uphill, went there, prayed and took the priest's blessings and continued his journey further on foot.

As he went further, he heard someone crying in utter pain. As he searched around, he found a man severely injured, near the bushes. Professor bandaged the man and used the medicines he had brought in his first-aid kit, to heal the man.

Professor nursed the strange man for a few days till he fully regained his health.

The stranger thanked him, "My name is Arjun. You were so kind enough to nurse me. I want to repay you by giving you a grand feast in my village nearby."

The Professor reluctantly agreed to him as he was a total stranger to him but just went with the flow. As they walked further, they reached the front gate of a village. There were two snakes in front of the gate.

By seeing them, the snake shape-shifted to human form and shouted, "Our prince has come back. Long live the Naga prince!"

Professor was dumbstruck at this strange sight and was about to fall unconscious, when Arjun supported the Professor from falling and told him, "I am the Naga prince. My name is Nagarjun. I am also capable of shape-shifting like the two snakemen."

He invited the professor to his village.

He introduced him to his father, "When I was ambushed and badly injured by the men of our neighboring rival village and was left to die bleeding, it was this Professor who came to my rescue and nursed me till I fully recovered. Because of the professor I am alive today."

Naga chief thanked the Professor, "Please stay with us for a while and give me a chance to repay your debt."

Professor agreed to the Naga chief and stayed a couple of days more in the Naga village.

There, Nagarjun showed the Professor that Nagamen could not only shape-shift from snake to human form, but also were blessed with control over the five elements (panchamahabootha). The Professor was totally fascinated by all this and requested Nagarjun to come to the city and experience the human world as well. Nagarjun agreed to the Professor as he was in Professor's debt as he had saved his life.

III

Nagarjun in the city

Nagarjun and the Professor bid farewell to Nagamen and came to the city. Nagarjun was astonished by seeing the human world filled with tall sky scraper buildings and four wheelers of different size and shapes. Technological advancement of the humans with latest gadgets and machinery left Nagarjun totally amazed.

Professor said, "Nagarjun, you can stay in my guest house."

Nagarjun kept watching television in the Professor's guest house and learnt a lot about the ways of the humans. Rest was taught to him by the Professor in due course. Professor took Nagarjun with him to places around the city on public transport buses, cabs and also on his scooter to city mall; hotels etc., and made him feel at home in the city. Nagarjun was happy and he had learnt to adjust with city life, though it appeared quite fast and busy and filled with pollution unlike his Nagavillage which was quite peaceful.

When Professor used to go for work, Nagarjun used to spend the day watching television. Sometimes he takes a stroll outside the Professor's guest house. One such day, Nagarjun was walking on the pavement in the city, he noticed two hooligans robbing a lady of her purse and jewelry by pointing a knife at her.

Nagarjun interfered and said, "Let the lady go. She had done nothing to deserve this."

The robbers laughed at him, "Move on if you want to live."

But Nagarjun couldn't turn a blind eye to what was happening. He stood in front of the lady blocking her from them. One of them tried to stab Nagarjun. He caught the knife and crushed it into pieces. He caught both of them by their neck high up in the air and threw them a mile away. They dashed into the garbage cans and ran for their lives.

The lady thanked him, "You saved my life. Thank you very much."

Nagarjun said, "You are welcome."

He went back to the Professor's guest house. Nagarjun was excited to tell the Professor on his way back from office how he had saved a lady from robbery. Professor was happy to hear this.

However, he told him, "Keep a low profile. Keep away from reporters and their camera, so that you can go unnoticed in the city."

That night, the professor made spaghetti for Nagarjun. Professor taught him to use knife and fork to eat spaghetti.

Nagarjun after eating spaghetti admitted, "The food in the city is quite delicious, but looks very strange."

Next day, Professor introduced Nagarjun to his next door neighbor Raghav, who was a kind of a loner studying in tenth standard in a school nearby as his parents are doctors in Dubai. The Professor used to take care of his daily needs. But he really missed his parents.

Raghav was happy to find a friend next door. He invited Nagarjun to play soccer with him in the field nearby. Raghav called his friends, made two teams. Raghav made Nagarjun his goal keeper. The opposite team was good at tackling the ball. They reached Raghav's goal post and were about to make a goal, Nagarjun kicked the ball all the way to the opposite goal post and made a goal. Raghav and the players were amazed at his strength.

Raghav appreciated Nagarjun, "Hey buddy, you have a lot of potential. You can be the next Ronaldo of soccer."

But Nagarjun had other things in his mind.

On their way back to the guest house, Raghav told Nagarjun, "You please wait here. I will get some vanilla ice cream for us."

As Raghav was crossing the road to the ice cream shop on the opposite side of the road, a truck came in high speed and was about to hit him. Nagarjun pointed his hand at Raghav and with his power made Raghav levitate high above the truck, saved his life and slowly brought him down to the road.

Raghav was wonderstruck and thanked Nagarjun for saving his life and asked him, "Are you a superhuman?"

Nagarjun told him, "No, not at all. Don't tell anyone about this incident. I am just a friendly neighbor."

After coming home, Nagarjun switched on the television. He saw news about a bank robbery happening in the town and that they had held many hostages at gun point.

Nagarjun immediately reached the bank. He kicked the front door open. The robbers started shooting at him. He had lightning speed and dodged all the bullets. He pointed his hand at their guns from a distance and the gun got twisted in shape and became unusable. The robbers tried to manhandle Nagarjun. But Nagarjun was beating and throwing them like pieces of vegetables here and there.

In no time, he immobilized the robbers, freed the hostages and vanished from the site. When the police came for rescue, they got bewildered by seeing all the robbers tied and lying unconscious on the floor. When the police enquired, they heard from the freed hostages about a mysterious superhuman with lightning speed and super strength and power. Soon the television channels were broadcasting about a mysterious super human. But they had no clue as to whom he was and where he came from.

The Professor came to know this incident, he congratulated Nagarjun and told him that he could do a lot for the city and be the savior of humans.

Nagarjun was happy with the newfound purpose in his life. Professor asked Nagarjun to accompany him on a flight to an excavation site. Nagarjun agreed as he was eager to fly on plane. They both boarded the flight from airport and when the plane was en route to their destination, the climate turned cloudy. It started raining heavily with thunder and lightning. The climate started becoming foggy and it obstructed the pilot's vision ahead. Though they were in constant touch with the air traffic control tower with their headsets, they lost their way in the fog and the plane got stuck into a cumulonimbus cloud. Each and every pilot feared cumulonimbus cloud as the survival rate of a plane stuck in cumulonimbus cloud was very dim. The plane would probably break into two halves.

All the passengers in the plane were totally panicked. The Professor asked Nagarjun if he could do something to save them. Nagarjun closed his eyes, concentrated his energy on the plane and created an invisible shield around the plane and maneuvered it through the cumulonimbus cloud safely without causing any harm to the plane and passengers. Then the pilot landed the plane safely at the destination.

The Professor took Nagarjun to the excavation site and made him familiar with the nature of his work. The professor gave Nagarjun few books to read on human culture so that he could find easy to mingle with them, while the professor worked at the excavation site.

Nagarjun kept himself busy reading books on humanity. By now, he acquired a good idea about human culture, their language and dialects of various regions. Just then the radio reported an earth quake of rector scale eight. Buildings and houses around started collapsing. People started screaming for help. The excavation site was all under piles of rocks. Nagarjun ran to the Professor's rescue. He moved the piles of rocks by just waving his hands from a distance. Professor was stuck under a pillar. Nagarjun pulled the Professor out. He was badly injured. Nagarjun held him over his back and rescued him out of the excavation site.

Professor told him to rescue the other humans. Nagarjun pushed the big boulder of rocks and debris away and saved humans who were stuck below them. Nagarjun brought the professor back to his guest house safely and helped him regain his health.

After a few days, Professor was back to his daily routine at the university. Nagarjun was again glued to the television as usual. He became fond of serials and didn't miss any of the episodes. On changing the channels, he saw a flash news about a fire breakout in a factory in the town. He immediately went to their rescue.

When he reached there, he saw all the factory equipments were up in flames. He, being a master of punchamahabauthic thathvas, concentrated his energy on the flames of fire, and within seconds he totally put off the fire in the factory. He brought the factory workers with harmful injuries to the hospital on time and was able to save many lives.

When the TV reporters approached him for his interview, he vanished from the site quickly. TV channels were all discussing about what had happened in the factory. The people of the city were thanking the mystery superhuman for his help in TV interviews. Professor was happy at what Nagarjun had achieved in such a short span of time in the city.

Rainy season was approaching. It started heavily raining in the forthcoming days. Climate remained cloudy. It kept raining with lightning and thunder constantly. Weather forecast in television warned of an upcoming flood in the area. Trees started uprooting. Water level in the sea was rising fast. People started losing their lives to severe lightning and thunder. The flood had started uprooting the trees and houses on its way to the city. Soon, the city was experiencing heavy floods. People were sinking in the disastrous flood. People were out of electricity and food supplies. Many fishermen were brought to rescue those who were sinking in the flood. Still they were running short of health workers.

Nagarjun was upset with what humans were going through. He sat into deep meditation, concentrated his energy on the flood and the climate around. He was able to calm the weather and flood with his energy and willpower. In a couple of hours, the flood disappeared and the weather became sunny again.

Professor was amazed at his abilities and asked him to share his knowledge of controlling the five elements to the world. Nagarjun had no notion to do so as this knowledge in wrong hands could result in total anarchy and destruction everywhere.

Nagarjun was becoming famous among humans, but no one knew his true identity. Digamber, a filthy rich businessman and also a bounty hunter was also keen to know the true identity of this superhuman, but for nefarious intentions. He wanted to capture Nagarjun, conduct experiments on him and somehow extract his DNA sequence to create similar super humans as slaves for him. He hired a private detective, offered him a lot of money to find the whereabouts of the superhuman. In the Professor's guest house Nagarjun was resting and watching television, when he heard news about a plane which was about to crash land due to engine failure. The nearby area was being evacuated to prevent any human casualty. Nagarjun got on a bike that professor had bought for him and rode to the evacuated area to see for himself. When he reached there, he could see the plane trying to glide safely and land down on the ground but was losing all its controls. Nagarjun levitated in the air with his power over the air element and flew in the direction of the plane crashing down. He stopped the plane in the midair with his bare hands, holding the plane's fuselage; he maneuvered the plane on his back and landed the plane safely on the ground.

IV

Dr. Binoy in Digamber's captivity

The spy had informed about Nagarjun's presence and location to Digamber. When the pilots and passengers thanked Nagarjun for saving their lives, Digamber showed up with his men to capture him. His men threw a net over Nagarjun and sprayed poisonous gas to make him unconscious but they were not aware that he was a snakeman and was immune to the poisonous gas. He tore the net wide open and spit poisonous venom on Digamber and his men to which they all fell unconscious.

By the time they woke up, Nagarjun was no more in their vicinity. Nagarjun, after reaching the Professor's guest house, told him about what he had gone through that day.

Professor cautioned him, "Lay low for a while. Gradually, the focus from you would shift to some other issues happening in some other corner of the world."

As told, Nagarjun remained confined to the Professor's guest house for a while. But Digamber's spy had followed him all the way to the Professor's guest house. He right away informed Digamber about Nagarjun and the Professor's connection. Digamber knew attacking Nagarjun in the guest house would be in vein as he will be too powerful for them to overpower and contain. He understood that the Professor was Nagarjun's weakness and decided to kidnap him to lure Nagarjun out. Early morning the Professor was on his way to the university on his favorite car. There was a tunnel ahead the road which the Professor used to cross on a daily basis on his way to the university. When the Professor rode his car under the tunnel, Digamber and his men were waiting for him there. They shot at the Professor's car and shot its tyres flat. They tied a cloth on the Professor's eyes and kidnapped him and took him to Digamber's hideout.

There, Digamber tortured him badly and told him to call up Nagarjun and tell him to surrender himself to Digamber, if he wanted the Professor to live. Nagarjun felt helpless and surrendered himself to Digamber in exchange for the Professor's release. Digamber's men from behind hit Nagarjun with a stick on his head to which he fell unconscious. Immediately Digamber's men captured Nagarjun, and immobilized him with tranquilizers. Digamber doesn't release the Professor, as promised, but kept on torturing him to find out if there were other Nagamen like Nagarjun and where did he find him. Digamber kept Nagarjun sedated in his private lab. He recruited a panel of doctors, genealogists and scientists from abroad to experiment on him to extract his DNA sequence to create super humans like him who could do his bidding. The doctors kept taking Ngarjun's blood and tissue samples from his body and performed all sorts of painful experiments on him. He became very weak and couldn't break out of Digamber's lab facility. Digamber's experiments were taking a deadly toll on Nagarjun and he was beginning to lose his life.

Digamber asked the doctors, "Why extracting his DNA sequence is taking so much time?"

One of the doctors replied, "Nagarjun is not human. He belongs to a unique species of Ichadhari Nagas which made it difficult to extract his DNA sequence."

Digamber shot the doctor who said this on the spot and warned the other doctors, "I want results and not excuses. You all will end up like your colleague. I am not spending millions of dollars for nothing."

On the other hand, the Professor was getting tortured on a daily basis but he kept mum about the Naga village and didn't disclose any other information regarding Nagarjun and his power. Professor was looking for a chance to escape from Digamber's custody. He noted the person guarding his cellar used to take a cigarette break in between when he would keep away from his gun and totally indulges in smoking. The Professor took advantage of the situation. He knocked the guard unconscious from behind, took his gun and key from his pocket, opened the cellar and escaped. Professor went to the lab facility which was situated nearby. Professor forced the lab security personnel to open the lab and let him enter by pointing the gun at him which he had taken from the cellar guard.

He saw Nagarjun tied to a bed in the lab with all kinds of wires and tubes connected to his spines and veins. Nagarjun was sedated and confined to the lab bed. The Professor, without wasting any time, removed all pipes and wires connected to his spine and veins. He tried to wake up

Nagarjun out of sedation by sprinkling some water on him. Nagarjun regained his conscious.

He said in a feeble voice, "I am too weak to escape. I am losing my life."

He continued in a sad voice, "I want to share something very important to you, Professor, before I breathe my last."

Professor came close to him.

Nagarjun started whispering into the Professor's ears. He disclosed the long lost secrets of the existence of Nagamani.

He told the Professor, "Nagamani has the power to bestow immortality to anybody who acquires it and keeps it close to his body by wearing it in the form of a ring or chain on his/her body. It also blesses the person with immense fortune and luck. The person with Nagamani will always win by stepping in any sorts of venture."

Nagarjun also mentioned about the Nagamani's medicinal properties.

He said, "It has the power to heal any incurable disease in the world. It would be helpful to everyone in the world."

Nagarjun also whispered the secret route to Nagamani cave.

But he warned the professor, "Nagamani cave is guarded by Ichadhari Nagas and they possessed control over five elements. Moreover, the Nagamani cave is filled with booby traps right from its start which requires one's mastery in controlling the five elements."

Right after disclosing the secret route to Nagamani cave, Nagarjun died instantly on his death bed.

Before the Professor could escape the lab, Digamber and his men held him captive and took him back to his cellar. When Digamber was disappointed on loosing Nagarjun, one of Digamber's guards handling the CCTV camera of the lab told Digamber that he had something important to share with him and took Digamber to the CCTV footage area. There he played the CCTV camera recordings of the conversation between Nagarjun and the Professor right before the death of Nagarjun.

Digamber got thrilled to hear the conversation about Nagamani and its power to bestow immortality, fortune and its healing powers. This was beyond just extracting the DNA sequence of Nagarjun. With the Nagamani's power, he could rule the whole wide world.

Digamber went to the Professor's cellar and told him, "Disclose the secret route to Nagamani cave."

Professor blindly denied, "Never."

Digamber tried to rope the Professor into disclosing the secret route to Nagamani cave by agreeing to share fifty percent of the profit with Professor that Digamber would make selling Nagamani in the black market. Professor denied his offer.

Digamber continued torturing the Professor hoping that one day or the other he would tell him the route to Nagamani cave. Professor tried to act unconscious after a bit of torture to get some lone time in the cellar. In the lone time, Professor started to write down the route to Nagamani cave in his pocket diary that he always kept with him.

During such gaps, the Professor succeeded to create a perfect map to the Nagamani cave in his diary, but he never showed it to anyone there.

Digamber told his men to intensify torturing the Professor as he was losing his patience. Digamber made use of lie detector to extract the truth out of Professor. He tortured him very badly, connected him with lie detector, and further tortured him to tell the truth. Professor was in a bad shape. He begged Digamber to stop the torture. Digamber kept on going with the torture as he thought that the Professor in a bad shape would crack open the truth any moment. To his bad luck, the Professor died of heart attack. Luckily, with the Professor's dead body, his wife got the diary from his back pocket. She kept it safe from others to hand it over to their son Vijay as and when he would return from the US.

Meanwhile, Digamber was totally frustrated as he had lost both Nagarjun and the Professor and was left with nothing. But he suspected the Professor's assistant Pooja might have some information regarding Nagamani or at least know something about where Nagarjun had come from and were there others like him and how to find them.

Digamber and his men waited for Pooja to leave the university premises after the office timings. Digamber's men pulled out a gun and told her to quietly come with them in their car or else threatened to shoot her. She was brought to the same hideout where the Professor was imprisoned.

Initially, Digamber asked her politely about Nagarjun and Nagamani. She replied that the Professor had shared no such information with her. Digamber didn't believe her. He told his men to start torturing her till she tells the truth. Pooja was going weary of the torture. She was too weak to withstand the torture anymore which Digamber noted. He finally said that he believed her and let her to go free.

Digamber didn't want her to die like the Professor as he will be left with nothing again. He had hidden intentions to free her. He called up the same detective he had hired to spy on Nagarjun and told him to tap her phone and keep him informed intermittently about her telephonic conversations. He said that he would wire transfer the money required for the purpose in his account.

V
Vijay in India

It was a chilly morning and as usual Vijay Nambiar had overslept and missed his exam of first year MBA in the College of Business Administration at the USA, Texas. Vijay was quite brilliant in studies but very irregular in attending college. In the college hostel, he was the one who cleared everyone's doubt and his hostel friends wondered why he kept bunking classes and exams as he was capable of acing any exam without preparations. From the past few days, Vijay had been working on his sports car, remodifying it all night. He was crazy about cars and racing. That day, at around half an hour to midnight, he got a message in his mobile with GPS location to an illegal car race which will be happening at 12.00 AM midnight. Vijay immediately geared up for the race, got his car keys and quickly escaped from the back door of the college hostel as all others were asleep at that time. He drove his car and reached on time for the race. Racers had blocked the road from one end to the other end. Everyone had started placing bets. The race began within no time. Racers kept crossing each other. Vijay with his modified car was still behind them. But he kept racing at a steady pace. One of the cars dashed the other car to head on, but instead, rolled over and crushed on the sideway. Vijay was catching up with the other riders but kept a distance behind the race cars so other racers were least bothered about him. But as the race was about to be over, Vijay pressed a button, switched on his NOS Cylinder fitted to his car. Within a fraction of seconds, he crossed all other cars and won the race and the bet money. It was middle of the night when he reached the hostel. He parked his car at a distance from the hostel quietly, making sure not to wake anyone up; he silently entered the hostel from the back door. Got to his bed, covered him up in blanket and slipped into a deep sound sleep, and slept like a baby.

Next day morning, he had overslept again and by the time he woke up, all his room-mates and others had already left for college. When he dressed up and was about to leave for college, his hostel warden came up to his room and told him that he could take the day off and was sad to inform him that he had just received a call from his mother in India informing the sad demise of his father, Dr. Binoy Nambiar.

Vijay was all in tears. He locked his room and called his mother home.

His mom cried, "Your father died of heart attack. Come soon and do the last rites of your father's funeral."

Vijay soon booked air ticket online. In no time, he boarded a flight of Indian Airlines from Texas to Cochin Airport. He hired a cab and headed straight home. He reached home to see his mother and family members mourning the sad demise of his father. His mother was all up in tears when she hugged him. He consoled his mother and started the funeral preparations and did perform all the last rites as being his father's only son.

After a few days, he decided to leave for Texas as he thought that there is nothing left for him there after his father's demise.

The very next day, when he packed his bag and was about to leave, his mother handed over him his father's diary and told him, "Your father wrote in the first page of the diary that he wanted you to have it after his demise. I forgot to hand it over to you because of the hangover of your father's demise. I am totally consumed by your father's memories."

Vijay dropped his bag immediately and took his father's diary to his room and quickly sat down to read the diary. In the diary, his father mentioned about NAGAMANI which had the power to bestow immortality and fortune to any human who kept it close to his body. His father first came to know about it when he was in an excavation site at Bhedaghat in Jabalpur, the heart of Madhya Pradesh which was also called the city of marbles. Near the waterfall in the Bhedaghat, he had found a tunnel in a cave with directions leading to the site of Nagamani. His father also mentioned that he had attached a map at the end of the diary which discloses the exact location of Nagamani and the last wish of his father for his son was to find Nagamani and acquire it. At once, Vijay decided to locate Nagamani as it is his duty as a son to complete his father's last wish.

Vijay called his father's assistant Pooja who was also an Archeologist. He needed her to accompany him on this expedition as the map was coded and Pooja who had worked with his father side by side had the skill and knowledge to decipher the map and could help him out in this mission as the cave mentioned in his father's diary was filled with booby traps and was guarded by Ichadhari Nagas (snakes which could take human form) who were deadly strong and their veins were filled with venom. Their bite in human form also is very lethal.

On receiving Vijay's call, Pooja was totally thrilled and got ready for the expedition. Pooja assured him, "I have local contacts here. I will meet you once you get here with the map."

Soon Vijay boarded a train to Jabalpur. As Pooja had promised, she was there to pick him up at Jabalpur railway station in her jeep. When Vijay was about to shake hand Pooja said, "Namasthe" with her hands folded.

She added, "This is not the US. This is India, man! You know, people here are very conservative and thus the greeting 'namasthe'."

Vijay also told 'namasthe' and got on her jeep to her residence.

Pooja remarked, "My jeep is not as fancy as your sports car but it is sturdy enough to withstand the pot holes on Jabalpur roads."

On the way to Pooja's home, the jeep was attacked by few mercenaries in an SUV, had shot her jeep's tyres and they went flat. The SUV crossed the jeep and blocked the road. The mercenaries threatened to shoot them if they don't reveal the hidden route to the Nagamani cave. Vijay had to hand them over his father's map as they were held at gun point and don't mind shooting them dead. They were trained mercenaries and had no conscious.

Vijay and Pooja reached their residence empty handed.

On reaching there, Vijay was stunned to see the outer skin of a snake hung on Pooja's drawing room wall.

By seeing him bewildered, Pooja consoled him, "Nothing to worry. It's the local belief here that hanging the outer skin of snake on the drawing room wall brings fortune to one's family."

Vijay heaved a sigh of relief.

He asked her, "By the way, how did they come to know about the map and that it was with me?"

Pooja replied, "Your dad was a famous Archeologist. When your dad made the map, rumors had already spread regarding Nagamani's existence. Your dad had somehow survived some attacks on him for disclosing the route to the Nagamani cave by various bounty hunters and mercenaries. But a very cunning bounty hunter Digamber, who is also a filthy rich business man, was after your father. Your father was threatened many times by Digamber for disclosing the hidden route to the Nagamani cave. But your father denied his offers of lump sum amount of money for the location of Nagamani. Your father was kidnapped by Digamber and tortured for several days in an isolated place. But instead of giving any information about the route to Digamber, your father died of heart attack. It was probably Digamber's men in SUV who stole our map."

Pooja lodged a complaint about the attack on her jeep at the nearby police station. On enquiry, the police found that Pooja's phone was being tapped by someone since Dr. Binoy Nambiar's death.

Pooja looked at Vijay in disappointment and said, "Now the map is stolen. All hope is lost."

Vijay consoled Pooja, "Don't panic. I have by hearted the map with codes, on my way to Jabalpur in train itself. The journey was a bit lengthy and boring. So I had nothing else to do to pass time."

Pooja was again filled with joy and optimism.

She asked Vijay, "Can you redraw the map you have memorized?"

Vijay said, "With pleasure."

He got down reproducing the map on a piece of paper given to him by Pooja. He did reproduce the map exactly.

He told Pooja, "Though I tried hard I could not decipher the codes on the map."

Pooja said, "Let me give it a try."

She got the map and started studying the codes for a couple of days. By the end of the week, she had totally deciphered the map.

Pooja said, "We need to hire muscle to counter Digamber and his men."

Next day morning, they geared up with all equipment, food supply and also recruited Bhima who was an ex-military and now a mercenary for hire. He was huge in size, quite muscular and was trained in Kickboxing, Taekwondo, Muay Thai, Krav Maga and weapons combat and was a sharp shooter when he was in the army.

He greeted Vijay, "I am a big fan of your father's work. Back in the old days, I had opportunity to work under him."

Vijay was happy to meet Bhima who was a contemporary of his father. As per the map, they had to head deep into the Kanha National forest reserve of Jabalpur where the Nagamani cave was located. They disguised as tourists with fake Id's and entered the Kanha forest reserve. They had to be careful as the forest was home to ferocious animals like leopards, tigers, reptiles etc. On the other hand, they had to handle Digamber, who was far more deadly than the ferocious animals and might have already reached the jungle.

In Pooja's jeep, they started travelling in the dense forest Kanha. Pooja had her GPS in situ to be on right track. Bhima was on guard at all times at the back of the jeep. It was a dark night, so they stopped driving the jeep and fixed up tents nearby. They collected some log of wood and lit a small fire. Pooja was feeling cold. Vijay put his jacket over her shoulder. She blushed and accepted the jacket as it was too cozy. They had sandwich, discussed about their journey ahead and then went to sleep.

After a while, Vijay heard a hissing sound in Pooja's tent. He came out and checked Pooja's tent. To his surprise, he found a huge python lying right next to Pooja. Pooja was in deep sleep and had no notion of a python lying next to her. Vijay got hold of a stick and pushed the python outside her tent. Python got agitated and was about to bite Vijay, Bhima came from behind and grasped the python's neck with bare hands. The python wrapped itself around Bhima and started compressing him. Bhima jumped and rolled over the ground with the python and got himself unwrapped from the python. Suddenly, Bhima took out a Swiss army knife from his pocket and stabbed the python on its head and killed the python. In the process, Pooja had woken up by the noise and was dumbstruck by seeing the dead python.

Vijay asked Bhima, "How will we dispose of this python?"

Bhima said, "No need sir, the python is huge and its flesh is very tasty. It will come in handy as food when our food supply will come short."

Vijay felt nauseated on hearing that and told Bhima to drop that idea as he is a strict vegetarian. They all had a laugh and went to sleep.

Next day morning, they went further on their route. After reaching a distance, the jeep's tyres had all got punctured due to the uneven path of the jungle filled with rocks and green thick bushes. Pooja said that they had to leave the jeep behind and cover the terrain on foot. Pooja, Vijay and Bhima got their back packs on and started walking under the scorching heat of Kanha forest. After covering some distance, they came across a marshy land covered with thick bushes all around.

Bhima told, "Take out your long knives and keep cutting the bushes ahead while walking forward."

After a while, Vijay started screaming in utter pain. Pooja came near Vijay and found nothing wrong with him. Bhima told him to take off his shirt. When he removed his shirt, they were shocked by seeing his body covered with leaches which kept sucking his blood. Pooja tried pulling them out but they held on sucking Vijay's blood. Bhima took out the turmeric bottle from his back pack and sprinkled turmeric all over Vijay's body. Slowly, one by one, the leaches came off his body.

Vijay asked Bhima, "I think leaches are allergic to turmeric."

Bhima said, "It makes them vomit blood. They cannot hold on to your body."

Then Pooja bandaged Vijay which reduced his pain. They kept going and after covering the marshy land, they reached solid ground. When they just stepped on the ground, they got cornered by Digamber and his men. Digamber's men were armed with knives and spheres. Bhima, Pooja and Vijay got into a fierce fight with Digamber and his men. Bhima, being an ex-military, knocked off two of the mercenary men of Digamber with just a double round flying kick. Vijay also knew a bit of street fighting, threw a couple of punches on Digamber's men. Digamber being cunning got around the back and pointed a gun behind Pooja and demanded Vijay and Bhima to stop fighting or else he would shoot Pooja. Digamber and his men captured Pooja and warned that he would shoot Pooja if they followed him. After Digamber reached his hideout, he gave Pooja the stolen map and threatened Pooja to decipher the coded map by next day morning or he will behead her.

In the middle of the night, Vijay and Bhima reached Digamber's hideout. Bhima and Vijay hit the guards on their head with iron rod and knocked them down unconscious. Vijay got inside the tent where Pooja was tied to a chair. He untied Pooja and rescued her from Digamber's clutches.

Next day morning, Digamber was disappointed at the present scenario and shot down his two men who were given the responsibility of guarding Pooja. By now, Vijay, Pooja and Bhima continued their journey ahead. As per the map, they had to cross a river upfront. Pooja saw a boat on the shore with a sign 'to hire'. She along with Vijay and Bhima went up the boat and enquired the charges to hire the boat. The captain of the boat was greedy and demanded double the normal price for hiring the boat for crossing the river, as he knew, whoever comes for hiring the boat were after Nagamani and were loaded with money which he craved a lot. Finally, Vijay agreed with the captain's rate as he had brought some cash stashed in his back pack that he got by winning illegal races in the US. Soon they boarded the boat for crossing the river. Little did they know that the captain of the boat was also after Nagamani and had spent years searching for it in the Kanha forest. The captain asked to have a look at their map so that he could steer the boat correctly in the right direction. Pooja denied the captain's request and told him that she had GPS and was well versed with the map and he just had to follow the directions she would give. She was a bit suspicious about the captain from the beginning. The climate was sunny and the boat kept cruising ahead the river.

In the meantime, Vijay and Pooja took some kickboxing lessons from Bhima below the deck of the boat. After they all got tired of practicing kick boxing all day long, they took a break and got sight of a bottle of rum at the corner. Three of them had rum and were wasted. They all dozed off the night. Next day morning, they woke up from their hangover and experienced a bit of morning sickness. Pooja who was not used to drinking, vomited a couple of times, then she was alright. They came above the deck of the boat. Bhima cooked them some sardines and salads and they had their breakfast. It was almost noon, when out of nowhere, Digamber's boat attacked them from the side and took them by surprise. Digamber's men started to shoot at them but Bhima was totally prepared for such a moment and came heavily prepared with hi-tech artillery. He handed over Vijay and Pooja both automatic imported gun and they started firing back. The firing went on for a while. Then the captain of the boat threw a grenade on Digamber's boat and it totally got blown into pieces.

Bhima asked the captain, "How could you get grenade in the boat?"

The captain said, "I was a pirate before I became a captain. I have knowledge of ballistic weapons like you."

The captain added, "I know about Nagamani and want to be a part of the mission."

Pooja denied the captain's request, "We are not after Nagamani. Our motive for the expedition is purely Archeological. We don't mean to profit on selling Nagamai in the black market like you."

They bid farewell to the captain once they reached the other side of the river. From there they continued their journey further. The forest became more dense and frightening as they continued with the map. They could hear the sound of wild animals close to them. They kept on going with a torch in each of their hands. Pooja kept wondering how Digamber was catching up on them without deciphering the coded map. She guessed, probably, Digamber might have hired an archeological expert for deciphering the coded map.

Anyways, she wanted to beat Digamber on finding Nagamani. They kept on moving forward the dense terrain. Sounds of wild animals approaching them became further close. A tiger pounced in front of them ready to devour them as his meal.

Bhima told everyone, "Stand still. Don't make any sound."

The tiger kept roaring at three of them with its mouthwatering.

Bhima told Pooja and Vijay, "Run as fast as you can. Don't do the mistake of looking back."

Meanwhile, Bhima climbed a tree next to him and the tiger had started chasing Pooja and Vijay with lightning speed. Bhima took his shoot gun and aimed at the tiger chasing behind them. The tiger decided to devour them and pounced at them. With haste, Bhima shot the tiger on its belly and it fell helplessly on the ground bleeding to death. Bhima climbed down the tree and was about to shoot the tiger again which was bleeding on the ground. Vijay stopped him from doing so.

He argued, "The tiger is also a living being. It has all rights to live on this earth just like us."

He pulled out the bullet from the semi-conscious tiger and bandaged it softly and left it to heal there itself. After everyone cooled down, they continued with their journey.

VI
Vijay in the Naga Village

As per the map, they were supposed to climb up a hill ahead. The hill was slippery. They had to use their trekking equipment to climb up the hill slowly. Many plants and shrubs grew on the hill. The hill was full of poisonous snakes. They carefully climbed up the hill avoiding the snakes. Vijay screamed on climbing a branch on the hill. He was bit by a poisonous snake. By then they reached the top of the hill where there was a temple. Bhima and Pooja helped Vijay up the hill. Bhima carried Vijay on his back to the temple, asked the temple pundit to help them out. One of the pundits was also a healer. He immediately tied a cloth like tourniquet on the hand of Vijay where he was bitten, which would slow down the spread of venom in his body. He recognized the bite mark on Vijay's hand and called for his assistant pundit to get a particular herb from the hill which would act as the antidote to the particular snake venom. Vijay had started turning pale. By this time, the pundit's assistant brought the herb. The healer pundit inspected the herb and ordered them to grind it and apply its paste on the bite mark on Vijay's hand.

By next day, Vijay was completely healed and felt ready to continue the journey. They thanked the pundits and asked for their blessings to fulfill their quest. Then they continued further as per the directions on the map. On covering further terrain, they reached a small hidden village up in the hill in the dense forest of Kanha. The village was beautifully covered with small huts all around. When they were approaching the village, two snakes blocked their way opened their hood and stood right in front of them. Bhima pointed a gun at the snakes and when he was about to shoot them, the snakes took human form and one of them crushed Bhima's gun with his bare hands. The other snakeman spitted poisonous venom like gas on three of them and they all become unconscious and fell on the ground. The snakemen captured three of them and brought them to their snake chief. The snake chief was angered at the sight of humans.

He shouted, "How dare you humans enter our sacred village and disrupt the peace which prevailed here from thousands of years?"

He ordered the snakemen to imprison them in a cellar deep in the village. After sometime, Vijay, Pooja and Bhima got back to their senses. To their horror, they found themselves imprisoned in a cellar guarded heavily by snakemen. They could notice them shapeshifting from snake to human form at will which shook them to their very core. The chief was benevolent on them and gave them food and water intermittently to survive. Vijay overheard the guards saying that the chief had ordered them to behead the humans soon, as the Naga village had to remain hidden from the human world. Vijay got petrified by hearing this and told Pooja and Bhima about the chief's order against them.

It was noon time when the guards had heavy food and were dozing off a bit. Bhima saw them in their drowsy state and realized it was the right time to escape. Bhima got hold of both of their neck from behind and compressed their neck till they fell unconscious. Vijay took the key out of their pocket from behind and opened the cellar and they ran to escape.

The village chief was busy conducting a competition among snakemen to find out who is worthy enough to marry his daughter. For doing so, the snakemen have to defeat the chief's majestic tiger in one to one battle. Among the snakemen, whoever could defeat the tiger in the battle would be considered worthy to marry the chief's daughter.

The chief's daughter is Rukmini. She is quite glamorous. One glance at her, that's all, it takes to make anybody's heart beat faster and every snakemen desired to marry her.

The chief announced, "Whoever defeats the tiger would not only get to marry Rukmini, but also qualify to be the next chief in command of the village."

The Nagaguru blew a trumpet and announced the commencement of the competition. Though the snakemen were huge and powerful, they kept getting devoured by the chief's tiger one by one.

The chief was totally disappointed with his men and asked, "Is there no one mighty enough to defeat the tiger?"

Right at this moment, Vijay, Pooja and Bhima were slowly escaping from behind the bushes around the circle where the deadly competition was going on. One of the snake guards got site of them and caught them red handed escaping and brought them in front of the chief. The chief got furious by seeing them. He declared that they had to face the tiger in the circle to survive. Vijay told Pooja and Bhima that he would go first to face the tiger as it was on his request that they had embarked on this perilous expedition which now seemed to be a means to their end.

Vijay entered the circle shivering out of fear. He was about to collapse by seeing the tiger approaching him. To his amazement, the tiger bowed down on the ground and started licking his feet. Vijay noted a scar on the tiger's belly and soon realized that it was the same tiger that he had saved from dying back in the jungle by removing the bullet from its belly and nursing it. He realized that he just got lucky and thanked God in his mind. The village chief was amazed at this strange sight and also a bit scared as Vijay had showed capability of taming a ferocious tiger with just his glance.

Nagaguru suggested, "Though Vijay is a human, he defeated the tiger and should be married to the Chief's daughter. It is the custom which we followed from thousands of years."

The village chief agreed with Nagaguru and announced the marriage of his daughter Rukmini with Vijay. Vijay was charmed by Rukmini's beauty and agreed to the marriage instantly.

After their marriage, Vijay asked Rukmini's and the chief's permission to go after Nagamani as it was his father's last wish. Rukmini realizing how serious Vijay was about finding Nagamani, requested her father to allow them to do so. The village chief agreed but told Vijay that he had to first learn to master the five elements (panchamahabhootha), if he ever wants to obtain Nagamani.

The Nagamani cave is heavily guarded by Ichadhari Nagas who were masters in controlling the five elements and the Naga cave is filled with booby traps which require one's mastery in five elements to overcome this. The village chief advised Vijay to undergo training of mastering the five elements under Nagaguru before he goes after Nagamani.

Nagaguru promised, "Vijay, I will teach you everything I know about Panchamahabhootha. But controlling the five elements requires hard training, immense dedication and sadhana."

Vijay agreed, "I am willing to follow whatever you say, guru."

Nagaguru was happy to hear this and told Vijay, "Come to my hut tomorrow at brahmamuhoortha (4:00 AM) to begin the training."

Vijay obediently reached Nagaguru's hut at 4:00 AM. Nagaguru first started teaching Vijay to meditate. After meditating till noon, Nagaguru asked Vijay to come to the ground. There Nagaguru by pointing his hand on a huge boulder of rock moved it above the ground in the midair without touching it. Viajy was amazed at seeing Nagaguru perform such anomaly.

Nagaguru said, "Now it is your turn to move the rock without touching it."

He tried with all his might but he could only move a few steps. The rock remained rock steady.

Nagaguru told Vijay, "You need more sadhana (contemplation). You further have to learn to feel the "prithvi" element within the rock without touching it. You have to work on your meditation and increase your willpower."

Nagaguru further said, "It is enough for today; go back to your chamber and take rest. We shall continue the training tomorrow."

Pooja and Bhima were eagerly waiting for him to know the outcome of his first day of training.

Vijay told them, "Mastering the five elements is not a piece of cake. It requires rigorous training."

Pooja and Bhima said, "We are also ready for it. We want to undergo the training."

Next day, Vijay along with Pooja and Bhima went to Nagaguru and requested for their training. Nagaguru immediately involved them in the training procedure.

As usual, the training began with hours of meditation practice. By noon, Nagaguru's disciples offered them some food to eat. After eating and taking some rest, Nagaguru called them again to training. Nagaguru instructed one of his disciples to demonstrate a form of 'Kata' (martial arts) specifically meant for gaining control over prithvimahabhootha. The 'Kata' involves a series of martial art moves which was very straining and tiresome. Nagaguru instructed Vijay, Pooja and Bhima to practice this form of 'Kata' till sunset.

By evening, they were totally exhausted. Their body was aching severely. They were given a decoction to drink to ease their pain. Nagaguru ordered the royal cook to grind and mix a few potent herbs in their two meals which would increase their strength and stamina at par with the Ichadhari Nagamen.

Now, their daily routine of five elements training included mastering martial arts and facing Nagamen in duel fights. In the initial days, they used to get beaten a lot but slowly, Vijay, Pooja and Bhima after learning some 'Katas', developed fighting skills and started to defend themselves well against Nagamen in duels.

After weeks of practice, Nagaguru told them, "It is time for you to initiate your final step in gaining full control over prithvimahabhootha. For this, you will have to stay buried underground and meditate for a period of thirty days. After accomplishing this you will gain full control over prithvimahabhootha."

Vijay interrupted Nagaguru, "How are we supposed to breath underground?"

Nagaguru tied a knot on Vijay, Pooja and Bhima's wrist and told them, "The knots are enchanted with mantras and it will help you to breathe underground. But you have to maintain your meditation without fail for a period of full thirty days to attain full control over prithvi elements."

Nagaguru ensured that area where they were buried remained isolated for a period of thirty days.

In the coming days, there happened to be a landslide in the village. But Vijay, Pooja and Bhima didn't get distracted from the impact of landslide and successfully completed their period of buried meditation for complete thirty days. After the end of thirty days, Nagaguru came with his disciples to the isolated buried site.

He ordered his disciples, "Dig them out of the ground safely."

After they were dug out, they were cleansed of the mud stuck to their body. Nagaguru chanted a mantra and united their knots.

He told his disciples "Bring them each a huge boulder of rock."

He then instructed Vijay, Pooja and Bhima, "Imagine being one with the prithvi element of the rock and try to lift the rock with your willpower without touching the rocks."

First Vijay gave it a shot. He closed his eyes, pointed his hand at the rock and imagined to be one with the rock and moved his hand upwards. To his amazement, the rock floated in the midair when he opened his eyes.

Next it was Pooja's turn. She closed her eyes and attempted the same. Similarly to her shock, she too had lifted the rock in the midair without touching it.

Now it is Bhima's turn and he closed his eyes and to his surprise, he too achieved the capability of floating the rock in the midair without touching it.

Nagaguru said, "I am glad to inform you that all three of you have achieved full control over prithvi element. Now you can move heavy solid substances made of earth element with your mere willpower. Tomorrow you can start your training over Aap mahabhootha. That is water element. Now you can take the remaining day off."

Next day, all the three had come on time at brahmamuhoortha to start their training. Nagaguru made them meditate as usual till noon, and then took them to the seashore in their village. There he instructed them to perform 'Kata' in water till their neck level. In the coming days, Nagaguru taught them new 'Katas' in water, specifically meant for controlling the water element.

After a few weeks of training in water, they were made to face Nagamen in duels in the water. Slowly they learnt to overpower Nagamen in water and developed speed and agility like Nagamen.

Nagaguru came and told them, "It is time for you to undergo meditation under water for a period of thirty days."

He gave three of them enchanted knots to tie on their wrist which would enable them to breath under water and protect them from sea animals like shark, crocodile etc.

After taking Nagaguru's blessings, Vijay, Pooja and Bhima dived deep under water. On reaching the bottom surface of the sea, they started with their meditation, nonstop for thirty days.

After completion of thirty days of meditation, Nagaguru came with his disciples and brought Vijay, Pooja and Bhima above the sea level. Nagaguru again chanted some mantra and united the knots on their wrists. Now he instructed them to try their luck with water element. As usual, Vijay stepped in front of the sea and closed his eyes and held his hands facing a boat in the water. On opening his eyes, he realized he has created floods in water and was able to manipulate the boat in his desired direction. Pooja came forward to try. She closed her eyes and imagined similarly, and when she opened her eyes, she could also manipulate the sea water and the boat in her desired direction. On Bhima's attempt, he could do the same without much effort. Nagaguru congratulated them on gaining control over water element.

Next day at brahmamuhoortha, their training had started for controlling the fire elements. Likewise, Nagaguru made them to meditate till noon. He allowed them to have their meals and take some rest. Then Nagaguru called his disciples in front of them and told them to demonstrate a 'Kata' meant for controlling the fire element. The following weeks they were made to study many 'Katas' to control the fire element.

One fine sunny day, Nagaguru came up to them and told three of them, "You had come to your final phase of controlling the fire element which require you to lay on a bed of fully lit charcoal and meditate similarly for a period of thirty days non-stop."

Like previous times, Nagaguru tied an enchanted knot on Vijay's, Pooja's and Bhima's wrists which would safeguard their body from burning due to the fiery charcoals. Nagaguru's disciples had made three beds of fully lit charcoal ready for their meditation.

After taking blessings from Nagaguru, Vijay, Pooja and Bhima lay on their respective charcoal lit beds and began to meditate with closed eyes. After a period of thirty days, Nagaguru came with his disciples and woke them up from their meditation. Nagaguru chanted a mantra, united their knots and instructed them to try manipulating fire by placing heavily lit fire in front of them.

Vijay tried first and imagined various shapes in his mind and held his hands in front of the fire. To his surprise, he could create all those shapes in fire without touching the fire. Next Pooja tried to manipulate the fire with her mind. She could move the fire in the direction she pointed. When Bhima's turn came up, he could shoot small fireballs from the heavily lit fire. Nagaguru was pleased with their achievement.

Next day, three of them geared up for the training of gaining control over the air element. Nagaguru took three of them up a hill nearby. It was at a bit high altitude. There they were made to practice meditation and 'Katas'. They were trained with spears, knives and axes. After they were skilled at using knives, spears and axes, three of them had to face duels with Nagamen high up the hills.

Nagaguru then told them, "Go on meditation here for the next thirty days."

Nagaguru tied the enchanted knots on their wrists to protect them from the freezing cold up the hill.

After the span of thirty days, Nagaguru came with his disciples to wake up them from their meditation. Nagaguru told three of them to open their eyes. To their shock, Vijay, Pooja and Bhima were levitating high up in the air. Nagaguru told them to concentrate their mind to bring themselves down from levitation.

Now they have entered the final round of training of the fifth element 'akasha' (ether). For which Nagaguru brought them to a cave where they were taught 'Katas' and special moves. To control the fifth element, they endured many duels with the Nagamen for weeks together inside the cave.

Finally, Nagaguru dictated them to meditate for the next thirty days inside the cave without any distraction, whatever may come up. Nagaguru left his disciples to guard the cave from wild animals and other disruptions.

After thirty days, Nagaguru went to the cave and awakened Vijay, Pooja and Bhima from their deep meditation and congratulated them over gaining control over 'ether' the final and the last fifth element of punchamahabhoothas.

Now they were capable of entering and filling any space in the universe.

Nagaguru told them, "The next task is to be able to withstand Ichadhari Nagas' poisonous bite and the venomous gas they spit from their mouth. For which three of you had to endure the intake of snake venom in low doses on a daily basis."

Nagaguru instructed his disciples to take care of this matter.

On a daily basis, they were given small pieces of meat bitten by snakes. Vijay also turned a non-vegetarian for completing his elemental training. It was now six months that they spent in the Naga village.

VII

Vijay in search of Nagamani

Finally, Nagaguru gave them his blessings to continue their expedition further. Vijay took the chief's permission and his blessings and bid farewell to his Naga kanya wife Rukmini and promised to come for her after attaining Nagamani. He also promised to take her to the US once he had accomplished his father's last wish.

After attaining siddhi in panchamahabhootha, they continued their journey ahead, based on the route mentioned in the map. As per the map, they had more terrain to cover further Naga village to reach Nagamani cave in Kanha forest. The Naga chief had given them three horses to ride on their journey. The Kanha forest kept getting denser as they rode further distance.

Suddenly they heard firing towards them from air. It was Digamber in helicopter firing mercilessly on them from air. Digamber's men in jeep were firing right behind them. Vijay got down from his horse. He pointed his hands towards Digamber's helicopter and waved it downwards.

Suddenly the helicopter pilot lost all his control. It experienced a severe turbulence and Digamber's helicopter crash landed down the hill. Digamber's men were still firing at them.

Pooja concentrated on their jeeps. She raised her hands up. The mercenaries' jeeps started to float up in the midair. Then she clapped her hands together with force which resulted in the mercenaries' jeeps dashing with each other in the midair and was broken into pieces.

Digamber's men got totally frightened and started to retreat. But there was Digamber's tank targeting them from a distance. It aimed and fired at them. Bhima was ready for the attack. He concentrated his energy and faced his palm upfront. The tank's fire propelled back in the direction it came from and hit the same tank. It blew up into pieces. Digamber had survived the crash landing and was planning to get back on them.

Vijay, Pooja and Bhima were content with their newly found powers which they mastered in the Naga village under Nagaguru's spiritual training.

After tackling Digamber and his men, three of them rode further. It was getting darker as they rode. So they decided to stop and camp. Three of them fixed their tents and lit bonfire and discussed their route further for the next day. Vijay had lit the bonfire but Bhima pointed his energy at it and the bonfire multiplied in its intensity and size. It gave them sufficient warmth. After which they wished 'goodnight' to each other and went to sleep in their respective tents.

Next day morning, the sunrise was very bright and the climate was also quite good for them to continue their journey. They packed their stuffs and got on to their horses and started riding ahead.

Digamber was always one step ahead of Vijay, Pooja and Bhima as he had placed a tracker in Pooja's watch when he captured her in the jungle and was on to them as usual. Vijay, Pooja and Bhima were totally exhausted as they had been riding the horses for a long time. Finally, they could view a cave at a distance. They got down from their horses and they reached the destination. There, they saw huge and muscular Ichadhari Nagamen guarding the entrance of the Nagamani cave. Vijay Pooja and Bhima started fighting with the Nagamen. These Nagamen were also well versed in controlling the five elements. Three of them used all the techniques they had learnt about controlling the five elements from Nagaguru at the Naga village. The fight continued till next day morning. They had been fighting the whole day.

By next day morning they finally defeated the Nagamen. When they were about to enter the Nagamani cave, Digamber and his men surrounded them from all sides. Digamber and his men knocked down Bhima and Pooja with a blow, with the rear part of their gun from behind.

He sarcastically laughed at Vijay and said, "I have been tracking you people all the while by placing a tracker in Pooja's watch."

Digamber pointed his gun at Pooja and Bhima and threatened Vijay that he would kill them both if Vijay fails to retrieve Nagamani from the cave. Vijay reluctantly went forward to get Nagamani for Digamber but for Pooja's and Bhima's safety. As Vijay moved forward, all the cave lamps lit by themselves and showed the way ahead. The Nagamani cave was very spooky. It was filled with spider webs of huge poisonous spiders. As he went further, blood sucking bats kept flying out of the cave. The cave was preserved from centuries by Ichadhari Nagas and they had ensured that no human ever entered the Nagamani cave. Vijay gathered all his courage to move forward. As he stepped on a stone ahead, a series of sharp axes started swinging at him from the sides of the cave. They moved to and fro like a pendulum. Vijay precisely calculated the rhythm at which the axes were swinging at him. He timed his footsteps accordingly and successfully came out of the booby trap.

He exhaled with relief and further continued his journey inside the cave. As Vijay stepped further, arrows started shooting at him from the sides of the cave. They looked very sharp and piercing. He moved with laser speed, caught those arrows on the way and broke them into pieces. As he moved forward, the cave's floor cracked wide open. There was quite a gap from his side to the other side of the cave. Below the gap were sharp and long needles pointing upwards. Even making a long jump wouldn't be sufficient to reach the other side of the cave. The sites of the pointy needles send shivers down his spine.

He sat down and meditated to activate the Vayu mahabhootha in his body and in the surrounding. After a while, his body began to levitate up in the air. He concentrated his energy within and literally floated in the air to the other side of the cave and evaded the pointy needles beneath the surface deep below. He gathered his courage and moved further ahead. The cave divided into three directions like a clueless maze. He was stuck for a while. He looked in the map, used his compass and went in the direction as per the map. As he went ahead, Vijay had to face fully lit fire throughout the floor to a distance up front. The fire was extremely hot, could burn him instantly if he entered the fire. The flames of the fire were up quite high, which made it difficult for him to jump above it. He decided to manipulate the fire, he pointed his hands on the fire, concentrated deeply on the agni mahabhootha and moved his hands apart.

Gradually the flames came down; the fire split apart and made way for Vijay to pass swiftly through the center of the path. As soon as he moved further, there started falling huge rocks and pillars from the roof of the cave. The rocks and pillars seemed quite heavy and could crush anybody to death. They were falling unevenly from the roof which made it difficult to predict where the rocks would fall next. Vijay closed his eyes and concentrated in his energy within and activated prithvi mahabhootha in and around him. When he opened his eyes, the rocks and pillars falling from the roof were all frozen in the air above. He walked calmly below the falling rocks and pillars. Next he had to face hacksaw blades coming out of the sides of the cave. They looked very sharp and had deadly zig-zag sharp curves. The blades could slice anyone instantly to death. Vijay prayed to Nagaguru for his blessings and tried avoiding the blades doing a series of somersault ahead the cave. Luckily he got through. At a distance, he could view the Nagamani kept quite high up a huge rock separated by a water body in front of him. He made use of his power of the five elements and walked over the water, reached the huge rock. The rock was quite high in size; he had to levitate himself up the huge rock, to see Nagamani in close proximity. It was glittering with an aura around it. He prayed to Naga God for his permission to take Nagamani and acquired it from its abode.

While Vijay was returning back, the cave started falling apart from the roof. Piles of huge rocks started falling all over. He, somehow, made it to the entrance where Digamber kept Pooja and Bhima in his captivity. He ordered Vijay to hand over him the Nagamani or suffer the consequences.

Vijay had no option but to give away the Nagamani to Digamber for the sake of Pooja and Bhima's safety. Digamber released Pooja and Bhima, as promised, and escaped from the cave.

Pooja, Bhima and Vijay too left the cave as it was falling apart. Three of them were very much upset as they faced all the risk and did hard work but Digamber got away with the prize 'Nagamani'.

VIII
Nagamani in Digamber's custody

Digamber kept low for a while. Then, with the power of Nagamani on his side, he began to establish his empire in the black market. He started smuggling and producing drugs like Heroin, Hashish, Cocaine, Flakka etc. and never got caught as the Nagamani kept protecting him. Soon he expanded his network of drugs overseas. Now, mostly everyone had got addicted to his drugs, mostly teenagers. He bribed the police and politicians to run his dark business smoothly. He also slowly started smuggling antiques around the world and sold them illegally in the black market. He started hiring more gangsters and gradually even the mob leaders also started to obey him out of fear. He hired professional thieves who had the skills to steal antique pieces without being noticed. He also got into trafficking girls around the world. He mostly roped them by offering job overseas and once they reached there as illegal immigrants, they had no option but to obey him. He forced them into prostitution. He killed some of them and sold their organs in the black market. He also got into printing black money. With the money he made by his dark business, he started investing in the real estate field. He started buying acers of land, started building up sky scrapers. He made a lot of money by then and he also started funding terrorism around the world.

The whole world was in chaos. Vijay, Pooja and Bhima decided that they will put an end to this. Bhima tracked down his drugs network with his military connections around. They came to know through his sources that a big consignment of Digamber's drugs was coming by ship that day. They got ready to nab the miscreants. It was almost night when the consignment arrived. Digamber's men were unloading the consignment of drugs when they got cornered by Bhima, Vijay and Pooja. Digamber's men tried using firepower against them but were all in vain as they were masters of the five elements. They easily destroyed their weapons and got into an empty hand fight with them. In no time, Vijay, Pooja, and Bhima overpowered them and handed over them and the drugs consignment to the police.

Digamber using his influence, got back his load of drugs from the police, but now he was aware of their interference in his dark business. He didn't bother much as he had Nagamani on his side to protect him from them. Vijay, Pooja and Bhima didn't lose hope on losing the consignment of drugs from police hands to Digamber. They decided to crack down his network one by one, expose him in front of the public and acquire their Nagamani back. Their next target was his professional thieves handling Digamber's smuggling of antiques. By now, Digamber had even bribed the Interpol officials for smuggling his antique overseas. This time, Digamber was smuggling his antiques as cargo shipment through air.

Vijay, Pooja and Bhima through their sources found about the exact time and location of the smuggling. For smuggling, Digamber bribed the airport officials. When Digamber's cargo was being transported from the hanger to the plane, three of them attacked the cargo loading section. They got into a bloody fight with the corrupt airport officials and defeated them in broad daylight, stopped the plane from taking off the runway. They informed AAI (Airport Authority of India) and DGCA (Director General of Civil Aviation) about the ongoing smuggling at the airport. The corrupt airport officials were arrested and were stripped of their jobs once for all.

Vijay, Pooja and Bhima celebrated their victory that night but Vijay told them that the war with Digamber is not yet over as he is into many illegal businesses around the world.

The recent kidnapping of the girls and the piling up of their bodies made the news everywhere in the TV. Though the parents of the girls had delivered the ransom money, the girls were still murdered. Their dead body was found devoid of internal organs.

Vijay, Pooja and Bhima realized that Digamer's organ trafficking racket was responsible for the recent happenings. Through Bhima's sources, they came to know about a hospital involved in illegal organ trafficking. The girls were sedated, brought by Digamber's men for surgical procedures and their organs were removed without their consent. After the operation when the girls revived, they were killed by Digamber's men and disposed of at isolated sites. Three of them decided to stop Digamber's dirty business as early as possible. They started keeping track of the doctors in the black market. Without their knowledge, they tapped their phones patiently till the next illegal operation had to occur in the hospital.

Three of them hid themselves in the IP ward and waited for Digamber's goons to arrive. At around midnight, they arrived with the sedated girls on stretchers, laid them on bed in the IP ward of the hospital. Then they went to meet the corrupted doctors to get ready and start the operation.

Vijay and Bhima told Pooja to free the sedated girls in the IP ward while they tackle Digamber's goons and the black market doctors. Vijay and Bhima took them by surprise and gave them the most severe beating of their lives, tied them in the OT room and informed the police.

By the time they arrived, Pooja had revived the girls out of their sedation. The police took statement from each girl and handcuffed Digamber's men and the black market doctors. As now they had witness and proof against them, they will be behind the bars for a long time.

Next, they had to crack Digamber's prostitution racket. The pimps on his pay roll mostly used to target teenage girls in the orphanages. Once they kidnapped girls, there wasn't much enquiry for them. They also abducted girls from rich families and demanded heavy ransom. Even after the parents gave them the ransom money, they didn't return the girls, instead used them for prostitution. The pimps used to drug them slowly so that the girls wouldn't run away from them as they got addicted to drugs and couldn't handle its withdrawal symptoms. This way, their pimps kept their mouth shut and the police at bay.

Through Bhima's sources, Pooja and Vijay found out a store house underground, where the girls were kept hidden. Three of them attacked the store house in broad daylight, entered into a horrendous fight with the pimps and Digamber's gang members. The fight only got over by night fall.

They were badly defeated by Pooja, Vijay and Bhima's elemental powers. The girls were rescued by them. They made sure that the perpetrators were jailed for life. They also made arrangements for the girls at deaddiction center where they were treated for months together till they were out of the toxic effect of the drugs. All this didn't affect Digamber as he was also into printing black money. Black money was printed by note making machines run by his gang in a remote country. As he funded a part of the black money he made for terrorism there, he had their support and protection. His black money used to come hidden in trucks carrying spices and other goods which were imported to his destination through the border. At the LOC (line of control) he found hidden routes, caves and tunnels that he used for smuggling the black money. Once he succeeded in bringing the black money inside the country, he would get in touch with filthy rich businessmen and get them to convert his black money into white money by giving them good commission for every exchange. This was how Digamber was running a parallel government with the power of black money in the country. This was a big racket.

Vijay, Pooja and Bhima collected lot of evidence against them and handed over to the government which led the government to initiate notebandi. By this, not only Digamber, but all the black money dealers were caught by the government. The government also influenced the bank into disclosing the black money stashed in various accounts in the names of corrupt politicians and businessmen. Because of this, the secretly running parallel government with the power of black money came to a standstill. The economy was down for a while but overcame this strategically in due course of time.

It was Digamber's real estate business that three of them targeted next. Digamber had committed lot of forgery in owning acers and acers of land from poor villagers, which led to the suicide of many innocent villagers. The sky scraper buildings that he built were all on banned areas of construction which adversely affected the environment and the people living there. Moreover, the construction materials used by him were of very low quality. The sky scraper buildings he built in the city mostly collapsed even during construction which led to the death of many poor labors. When the labors asked for compensation, Digamber just turned a blind eye to them. He killed those who raised any voice against him with his gangsters who were on his pay roll.

Vijay, Pooja and Bhima found out that most sky scraper buildings were constructed at illegal sites. The acers of land Digamber acquired with his goons were based on forged documents. The poor villagers were tortured to sign on blank papers. Digamber's whole real estate business was fraudulent. They brought all this to the light of the police. They submitted the forged documents and stamp papers to the police. The poor villagers were assured protection by Vijay, Pooja and Bhima from Digamber and produced them as witnesses in the court. After thorough enquiry, as per the court order, the forged areas of lands were returned to their rightful owners who were the poor villagers who solely depended on land cultivation for their survival.

Immediately, Digamber's construction sites were prohibited from any further construction. The sky scrapers that Digamber already built were declared not safe for inhabiting and were brought down with explosives. His construction sites were all destroyed one by one, but Digamber didn't come in the open. He was still missing. The police issued an arrest warrant in his name in each and every police station but he managed to stay out of sight.

Vijay, Pooja and Bhima were on constant look out of Digamber. But he somehow stayed under the radar at all times. Soon they came to know about Digamber's illegal production of weapons. He received millions of dollars from terrorist organization to manufacture weapons of mass destruction without license. He also manufactured C-4, a very powerful remote controlled bomb which was in high demand in the black market. He provided terrorists with weapons of latest technologies which gave them advantage over policemen who were used to only normal rifles and shot guns. He also made ballistic missiles, bazookas, grenades and all sorts of latest weaponry available in the black market. His weapons manufacturing unit was located in another country. There he also funded for terrorist training and provided a safe haven for many terrorist organizations that were wanted by the UN and many other countries, though the US and many other countries had imposed sanctions on Digamber's weapon manufacturing country. They continued terrorism with the massive funding they received from negative elements like Digamber himself. Soon Digamber was wanted by the Interpol but they couldn't figure out where he was hiding.

Vijay, Pooja and Bhima went to his weapon manufacturing country in search for Digamber. There they found his weapons manufacturing factory and godown. The police and government were in total chaos. They were in no position to help them. They strategically attacked Digamber's base there. They went by nightfall, immobilized the guards there and blew the transformer connected to the factory. They got in like spies. They collected all the information and soft copies about all the countries the weapons were getting illegally transported. They confiscated the details of all terrorist organizations funding the manufacture of such lethal weapons, their training base and names. They located C-4 in the godown.

Vijay, Pooja and Bhima wired the whole factory and godown completely with C-4. After coming to a safe distance from the factory they pulled the trigger of C-4. Soon the factory and the go-down exploded with a bang. It was a treat to Vijay, Pooja and Bhima's eyes. But they failed to find Digamber there. He was safely operating his gang from somewhere overseas.

When they inspected the soft copies they got, they came to know Digamber's main source of money was through smuggling gold from Dubai to India, as Dubai was where the purest form of gold was available. It fetched him good money by smuggling gold to India. He was the kingpin of gold mafia in the Arab. A big share of the money he made by smuggling gold was used in funding his other crimes and terrorism around the world. He had hired gangsters whose expertise was smuggling gold through sea, hidden all the way to India. He converted pure gold into gold biscuits and filled them into containers ready for shipment via sea to India. His gold shipment was heavily guarded by armed gangsters in ship. He had bribed the officials of the shipyard for free pass there. He informed them about his contacts in India to get to the shipyard and pick up the shipment. This is how his gold reached jewelry shops in India, illegally, making lot of money in this process.

The Customs Department of India was fed up with Digamber and his men as his gold shipments made way to India frequently without being caught. Digamber had bribed all the officials from top to bottom whoever involved in the inspection of shipments reaching India.

His other means of smuggling gold from Dubai to India was via passengers of commercial planes from Dubai to India. He hired smugglers who were ready to stash gold in powder form in their rectum, to go undetected at the security checkup at the airport. If this didn't work, he bribed airport officials to help out in smuggling gold.

Digamber's men would hide the gold at the bottom of their bags or in their dress. Once they reached the airport, they would hide it in the airport toilet or some other location conveyed to them by the corrupt airport officials and go undetected trough security checkups at the airport. The airport officials under Digamber's pay roll then further ensure the safe transportation of gold hidden from the airport authority outside the airport premises.

Outside the airport, Digamber's men would be waiting in various vehicles to smuggle the gold from there, unnoticed, to various locations in India. Then it would be sold in the black market fetching Digamber loads of money making him filthy rich again.

Vijay told Pooja and Bhima to go and snatch his gold shipment coming from sea while he would catch Digamber's men red handed at the airport. Pooja and Bhima in a motor boat began to follow Digamber's gold shipment in the sea. They sneaked in on the gold shipment by nearing the motor boat to Digamber's ship. They used their power over five elements to beat Digamber's men on boat, captured his consignment of gold and handed it over to the police officials. In the meanwhile, Vijay had informed the A.A.I (Airport Authority of India) and the D.G.C.A (Director General of Civil Aviation) about the gold smuggling happening at the airport. There he was ready with Customs officials and police force at alert mode unknown to Digamber's men at the airport. There the corrupted airport officials and Digamber's smugglers were caught red handed by the police force instantly. Digamber's men tried to escape on reaching the airport but were surrounded by police and Customs officials and they finally had to surrender to the police.

Bhima's sources found out Digamber's location. He was hiding in Dubai and operating his gang in India from there. As there was no extradition treaty between India and Dubai, Digamber had a kind of immunity there and was enjoying his luxurious life there as a free bird.

Vijay, Pooja and Bhima realized that it is now only up to them to bring Digamber behind the bars. They booked their air tickets soon to Dubai and reached Dubai airport in Emirates airlines. Vijay, Pooja and Bhima stayed at a hotel near to Digamber's residence in Dubai. His mansion was held in tight security from intruders. He had fixed CCTV cameras in almost every location, had snipers on the roof of his mansion. His gang members were always alert and were armed with A K 47. Digamber had his chopper on the helipad on his roof to escape in case he is attacked.

Bhima first put the lights off. Then Bhima, Vijay and Pooja took Digamber's men by surprise. His men started shooting around but, Vijay, Bhima and Pooja maneuvered themselves from the bullets and defeated the guards in a fierce and brutal fight. Digamber ordered to get his chopper ready to escape, as quickly as possible, and reached the helipad on the terrace. Vijay, Bhima and Pooja had reached there before hand. They used their air elemental powers to destroy the helicopter before takeoff. Three of them got into a dreadful fight with Digamber and his bodyguards on the helipad. Digamber's bodyguards were no match to Vijay,

Bhima and Pooja's elemental powers. They killed his body guards and Digamber was now cornered. Though Digamber had Nagamani and all the luck in the world, he was devoid of elemental powers.

Soon, they overpowered him and removed the Nagamani from his body which he was wearing in a chain around his neck. He was now helpless and begged for their forgiveness as he is no more immortal without Nagamani.

Vijay said, "You are responsible for torturing my father to death. If I want, I can kill you with just a snap of my fingers."

He possessed elemental powers and no one in the world could question him but he wanted Digamber to accept his crimes and surrender himself to the Indian police.

Soon they took Digamber to India and handed over him over to the police with all the evidence they procured against him. The court sentenced Digamber to be hanged till death.

Vijay, Bhima and Pooja had finally brought justice to whomever Digamber had wronged.

Vijay, Pooja and Bhima were given Medal of Honor by the Indian government. Later, Nagamani was kept in a museum in tight security. Vijay, Pooja and Bhima went back to the Naga village. Pooja and Bhima settled in the Naga village. Vijay took his Nagakanya wife to the US and also completed his MBA from College of Business Administration at Texas, USA. He got selected as the CEO of a multinational company which specialized in manufacturing sports cars. The world was in everlasting peace and they lived happily ever after.

***

9 798885 460620